To
..... Celeste Taylor ......

MERRY CHRISTMAS

Love from,

...... Fiona Taylor ......

Santa is Coming to
VERMONT

Written by Steve Smallman   HOMETOWN WORLD   Illustrated by Reuben McHugh

"Well?"

boomed Santa to the head elf.
"Have all the children from
Vermont been good this year?"

"Yes!" said the elf. "From Middlebury to Montpelier,
from Rutland to Colchester, all the children in
Vermont have been very good!"

"Jolly good!" chuckled Santa:

"Then we'd better get their presents
onto the sleigh!"

Even though the sack of presents was
really, really big
and the elves were really, really small,
they seemed to have no trouble
loading it onto Santa's sleigh.

"We're ready to go to **Vermont!**"
announced Santa.

"Er...not quite," said the head elf:
"One of our reindeer is missing!"

MAP OF
VERMONT

"Missing?

Which reindeer is missing?" asked Santa.
"Comet, Santa!" said the elf. "I've called and called, but…"

Just then, a reindeer appeared, munching on a large carrot.
"There's Comet!" said Santa, giving the reindeer a little wink.
"Now let's go to Vermont!"

With a flick of the reins,
off they went, racing through the sky.

"Ho, ho, ho!" laughed Santa.

"We'll soon have these presents
delivered to the Green Mountain State!"

Santa's sleigh flew high through the
wintry air across the Arctic Ocean. In the
wink of an eye, the sleigh was flying
above Canada, and onward to Vermont.

Suddenly, the sky filled with clouds
and snowflakes whirled around the sleigh.
They were in a blizzard!

MAP OF
VERMONT

They couldn't see a thing and soon
seemed to be hopelessly lost!
Which way was Vermont?

In the midst of the howling storm,
Comet peered into the distance.
Was that Lake Champlain?
With a sharp tug, Comet started leading
the sleigh downward.

"Whoa!" cried Santa.
"What's going on?"

Down,
down,
down
they went.
Then, when the clouds parted,
Santa discovered exactly where they were...

They had reached **Vermont!**

"**Well done, Comet!**" exclaimed Santa.
"Now I know where we are.
Don't worry children, **Santa is coming!**"

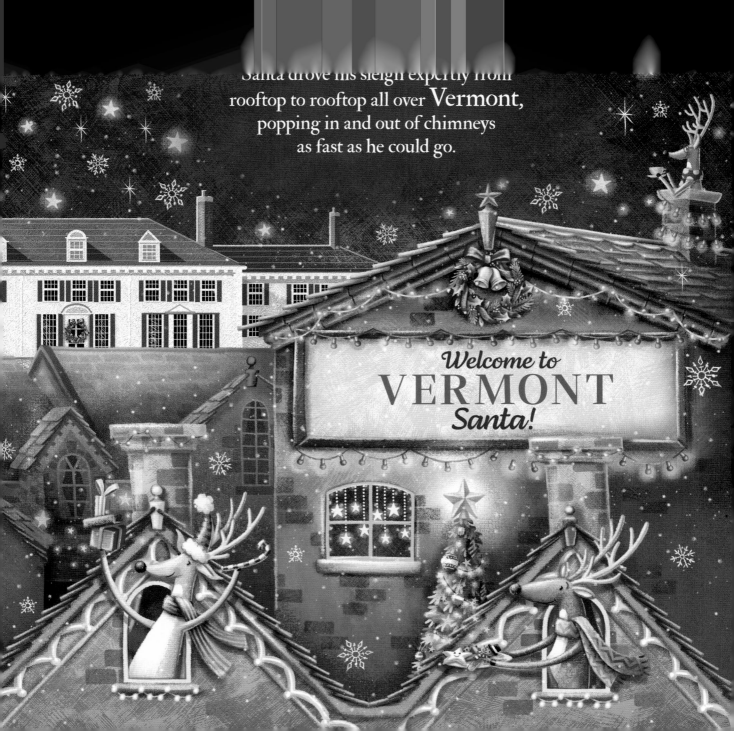

Santa drove his sleigh expertly from rooftop to rooftop all over **Vermont**, popping in and out of chimneys as fast as he could go.

Welcome to
VERMONT
Santa!

There were **big** chimneys in Burlington,

and *small* chimneys in Bennington.

Santa squeeeezzed down chimneys in Brattleboro,

and plummeted down chimneys in Barre.

In house after house all over **Vermont**,
Santa delved inside his sack for packages
of every shape and size.

He piled them under the Christmas trees
and carefully filled up the stockings
with surprises.

HOME SWEET
HOME
VERMONT

All the good children of **Vermont**
had left out a large plate of cookies, a small
glass of milk, and a big, crunchy carrot.

Santa took a nibble out of each cookie
and a sip of milk, wiped his fluffy beard,
and popped the carrot into his sack.

From Stowe to Shelburne,
from Essex to Milton,
Santa and his sleigh visited every house
in the Green Mountain State.

Comet was amazed at how quickly
they went. Santa never seemed to get tired
at all. But Comet was starting to feel a bit
sleepy and quite hungry, too!

Finally, Santa had delivered the last present
on his long **Vermont** list.

"**It's past midnight**," he sighed,
"...and my sack seems as heavy as ever!
I hope I haven't forgotten anyone."

Santa opened his sack to check...but it was full
of crunchy carrots!

Santa divided the carrots among all the reindeer.
"Great job!" he said, patting Comet gently on the nose.
But Comet didn't hear him...
Comet was too busy munching!

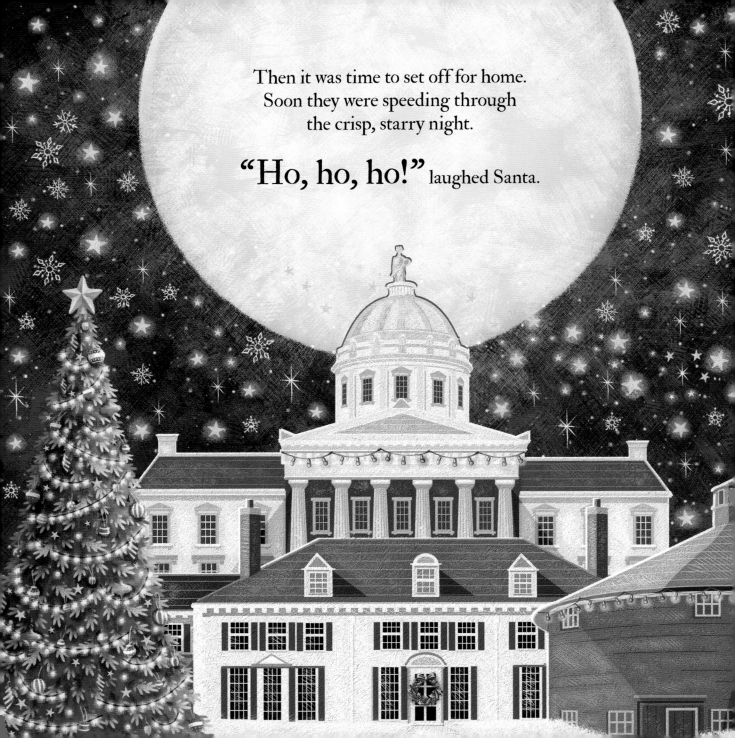

Then it was time to set off for home.
Soon they were speeding through
the crisp, starry night.

"Ho, ho, ho!" laughed Santa.

Written by Steve Smallman
Illustrated by Reuben McHugh
Landmark art by Jo Parry
Designed by Ryan Dunn

Published by Hometown World,
an imprint of Sourcebooks Kids
P.O. Box 4410, Naperville, Illinois 60567-4410
(630) 961-3900
hometownworld.com
sourcebookskids.com

Source of Production: 1010 Asia Limited,
Kwun Tong, Hong Kong, China
Date of Production: April 2024
Run Number: 5036158
Printed and bound in China (OGP)
10 9 8 7 6 5 4 3 2 1

HOMETOWN WORLD

Read local with the #1 bestselling hometown books for kids!

UNIQUE GIFTS for birthdays, holidays, and every day!

Choose from available locations in 50 STATES and SELECT CITIES.

Snuggle up with Hometown World because

NOTHING FEELS MORE LIKE HOME...than a good book!

Visit HometownWorld.com for more!